P. ZONKA

LAYS AN EGG

JULIE PASCHKIS

Ω
PEACHTREE
ATLANTA

Ω

Published by
PEACHTREE PUBLISHERS
1700 Chattahoochee Avenue
Atlanta, Georgia 30318-2112
www.peachtree-online.com

Design by Julie Paschkis; composition by Loraine M. Joyner

The illustrations were rendered in watercolor on 100% rag archival watercolor
paper. Titles and byline are hand lettered. Text is typeset in International
Typeface Corporation's Tiepolo by Cynthia Hollandsworth Batty and
was named for Italian artist Giovanni Domenico Tiepolo.

Printed in November 2014 by Tien Wah Press in Malaysia
10 9 8 7 6 5 4 3 2 1
First Edition

Library of Congress Cataloging-in-Publication Data

Paschkis, Julie.
P. Zonka lays an egg / by Julie Paschkis.
pages cm
ISBN 978-1-56145-819-6
Summary: "All of the chickens in the farmyard lay eggs regularly—all except for
P. Zonka, that is. She's too busy looking at the colors of the world around her.
The other chickens think P. Zonka's just lazy...until she lays the most beautiful
egg they've ever seen."— Provided by publisher.
[1. Chickens—Fiction. 2. Eggs—Fiction. 3. Color—Fiction.] I. Title.
PZ7.P2686Paaf 2015
[E]—dc23
2014006507

for Jan and Greg

Maud laid one egg every day.

Dora laid an egg every other day.

Nadine always laid exactly five eggs a week.

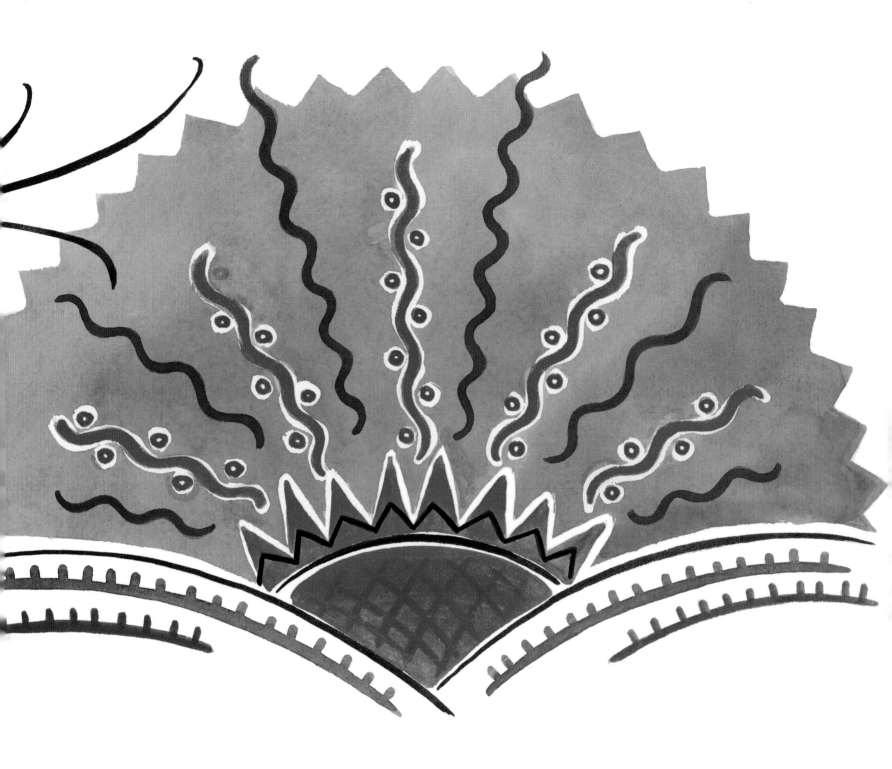

Gloria never laid an egg because
he turned out to be a rooster.
It was his job and he did it well.

All the other chickens
laid eggs regularly.

All of them except P. Zonka.

"Why doesn't P. Zonka lay eggs?"
asked Maud.

"Because she wanders around the farmyard
day in and day out, staring at flowers and
gawking at clouds," said Nadine.

"Oh tut-tut," clucked Dora.
"She's just a dreamer."

"Cock-a-doodle-doo!" said Gloria.

P. Zonka paid no attention to them.
She looked down at the shiny green grass
and gazed up at the deep blue sky.

"I'm quite good at laying eggs,"
Nadine said to P. Zonka one day.
"You never even give it a try."

"Look around, Nadine!" said P. Zonka.
"Look at those big red tulips and
the little pink cherry blossoms!"

Day after day, Nadine, Dora, and Maud
and all of the other hens filled baskets of eggs.

P. Zonka didn't lay a single egg.

"Why?" asked Maud.

"Please tell us why," said Dora.

"Why indeed?" clucked Nadine.

"Cock-a-doodle-doo?"

"I will tell you why," said P. Zonka. "Because of the pale mornings, the soft dark moss, the stripes on the crocuses, the orange cat with one blue eye, the shining center of a dandelion, the sky at midnight."

"I don't get it," said Maud.

"P. Zonka is just plain lazy," said Nadine.

"Come on, P. Zonka," urged Dora.
"You might like laying an egg."

"Cock-a-doodle-doo!"

"Can't you at least try?" they all asked.

P. Zonka thought for a moment.

She climbed slowly onto an empty nest.

Maud let out a nervous cackle.

"She'll never be able to do it," said Nadine.

"Oh my," said Dora.

P. Zonka fluffed her feathers

and flapped her wings.

She clucked softly to herself and sat down.

Flutter, flutter.

Cluck, cluck.

Nothing happened.

P. Zonka did it all again.

Flutter, flutter.

Cluck, cluck.

PUSH!

At last!

P. Zonka stood up and looked at her egg.

It wasn't a white egg,

a brown egg,

or even a gray-blue egg.

It was...

...Spectacular!

There were patterns of sun yellow, grass green, tulip red.

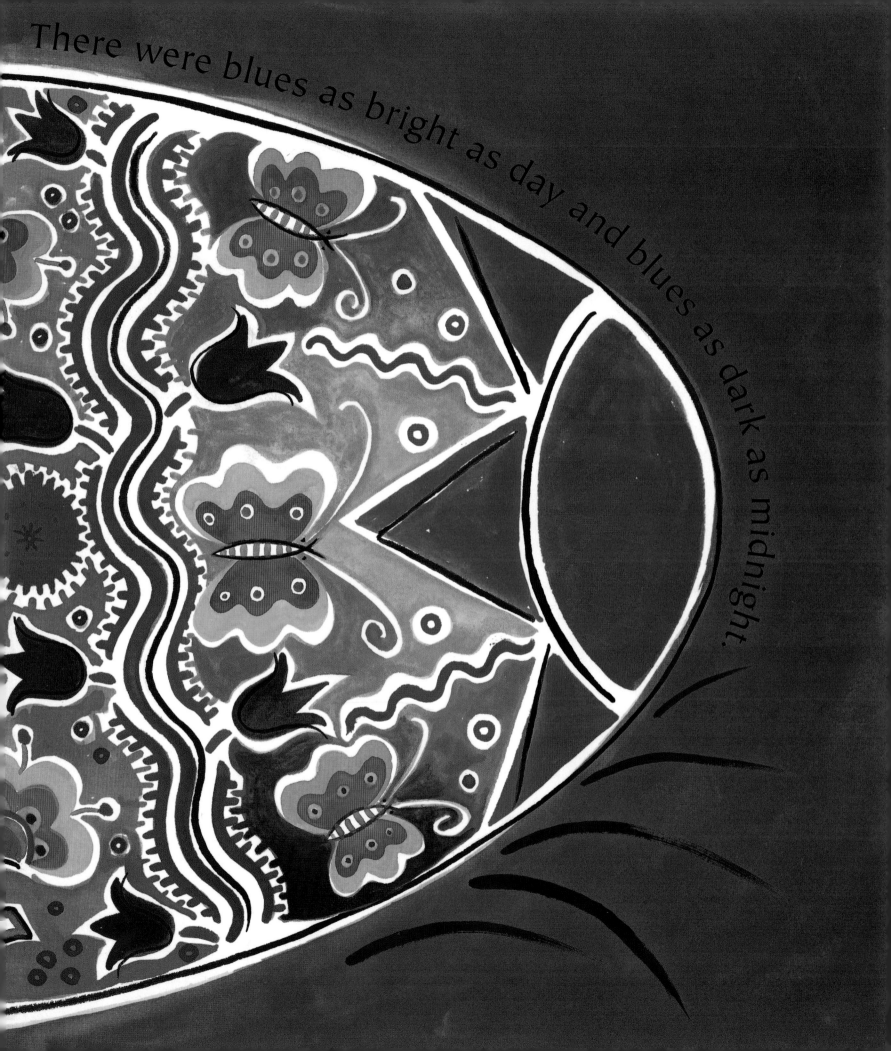

There were blues as bright as day and blues as dark as midnight.

"My goodness!" cried Maud.
"My stars!" marveled Dora.

"But is it a little too much?"
asked Nadine.

"Cock-a-doodle-doo!"

"This egg is beautiful,"
they all agreed.

After that,
P. Zonka went back
to wandering around
the farmyard. She looked
down and she gazed up.
She clucked in wonder at
all the colors she saw.
She didn't lay very
many eggs…

...but the ones she laid
were worth the wait.

A PYSANKA is a Ukrainian decorated egg made with patterns of beeswax and layers of dye. Many people all over the world decorate pysanky (the plural of pysanka). Every year Julie's sister Jan and her husband Greg have a big neighborhood party where friends and family decorate eggs and eat delicious food. The party is spectacular and this book came out of that experience.